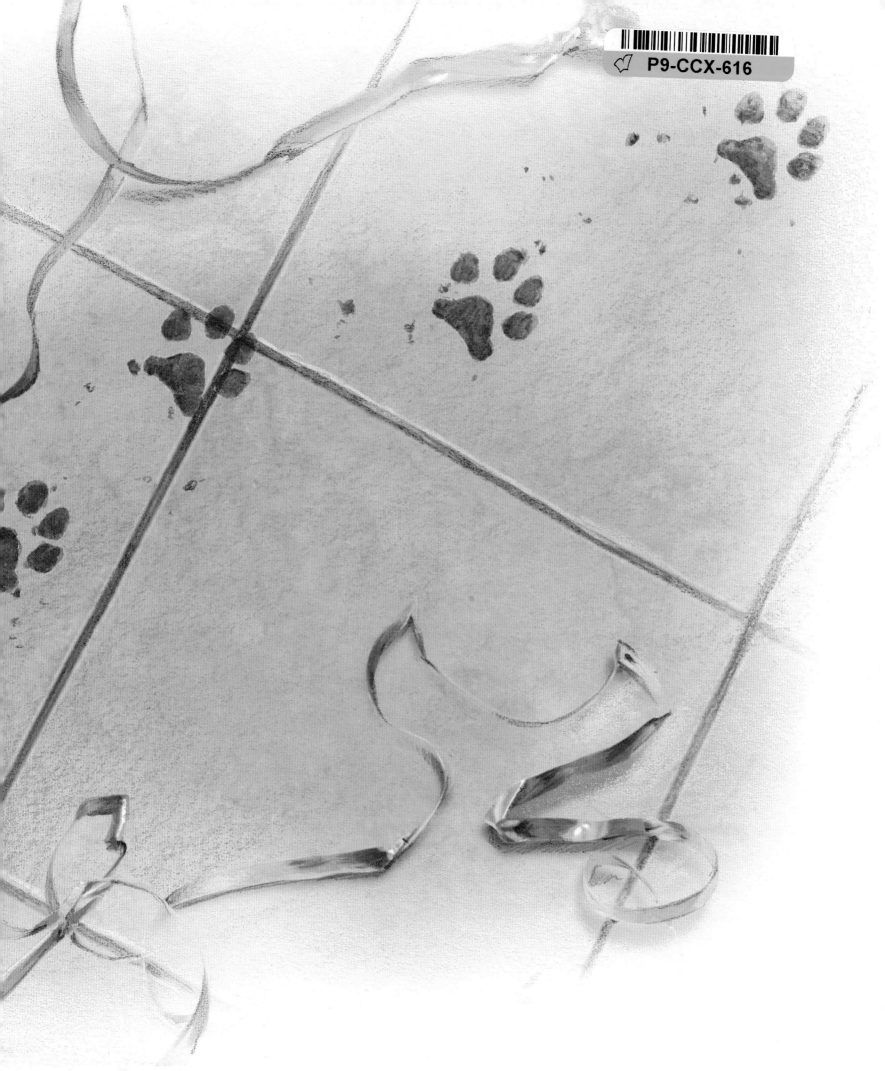

Written by Deborah Chancellor
Illustrated by Simon Mendez (Advocate)

First published by Parragon in 2009

Parragon
Queen Street House
4 Queen Street
Bath BA1 1HE, UK

ISBN 978-1-4075-6370-1

Printed in China

Muddypaws
and the
Birthday Party

PaRragon

Bath · New York · Singapore · Hong Kong · Cologne · Delhi · Melbourne

Ben was just a smallish, normalish boy, but he was Muddypaws' **best friend**.

They went out for the best ⸮ sρlishy-sρlashy ⸮ muddy walks together.

They made new friends together of all sizes, colors, and smells.

They did everything together.

But one sunny morning, Muddypaws woke up
to find everything had changed in his house.
There were lots of new things!

He sniffed around excitedly. What was happening?
Where was Ben? He scampered off to find him.

"WOOF!" barked Muddypaws, dropping his favorite ball at Ben's feet.

"Let's play!"

But Ben was busy playing with a strange shiny thing. And the strange shiny thing was getting bigger ... and bigger ... and BIGGER!

Ben's new game looked like fun! Muddypaws pounced on the mountain of strange shiny things...

Bang! Muddypaws jumped away as fast as he could. He didn't like that game! But what was that delicious smell coming from the kitchen...?

His tail began to wag. Sausages!
Surely no one would mind...

... if he tried a little one? But someone did mind!

"Bad dog!"
scolded Ben's mom,
and shooed him outside.

Muddypaws' tail stopped wagging. Why didn't Ben want to play with him? Why was everything different today?

Maybe Honey the cat would want to play. "WOOF!" barked Muddypaws. "Let's play!" Honey turned up her nose.

She had better things to do than play with a puppy—
like rolling on the grass in the sunshine!

Then the gate squeaked open...

...and the front yard was filled with stamping feet, new smells, and loud voices.

A crowd of children ran up the path into the house.

Something interesting was certainly going on—and Muddypaws was stuck in the yard with no one to play with.

The flowers were **boring.** The grass was **boring.** Even the smells were **boring.** And Muddypaws was getting hungry. He tried to find his bone...

...but it had disappeared.

What was happening inside the house? Maybe he would just look through the window to see.

Muddypaws pushed his nose up against the glass. Ben and the other children were running around and laughing. They looked like they were having a great time!

Muddypaws wanted to join in more than anything in the whole world.

Then Ben's mom walked into the room carrying something that was **twinkling** brightly.

It was the **biggest**, most **delicious** looking cake Muddypaws had ever seen, and it was topped with little lights!

Muddypaws licked his lips and pressed his nose
even harder against the window.
Suddenly the door opened.

It was Ben.

"Mom says you can come in now!" cried Ben.

But all at once, Muddypaws didn't want to come inside.

He didn't like the big shiny things that went **bang!**

He didn't like it when
Ben's mom shouted at him.

He wasn't sure about all the
new children in his house.

"I know what to do," Ben said.

Ben threw Muddypaws' ball high into the sky.
"Catch, Muddypaws!" he cried.

At once, Muddypaws forgot about
the big shiny things...
He forgot about the new children...
He even forgot about Ben's mom shouting...

Ben wanted to play with him!
Muddypaws jumped and barked for joy.
He ran as fast as he could to fetch his ball,
and brought it back to Ben.

Ben scooped Muddypaws into his arms and gave him a big hug. "I'm sorry, Muddypaws!" he whispered. "You didn't know it was my birthday. But you do know you're my best friend, don't you?"

"And best friends do everything together—especially sharing birthday treats!"

"WOOF!" barked Muddypaws.

"Sausages!"